ALBERT'S BIGGER THAN BIG IDEA

WITHDRAWN

by **Eleanor May** • Illustrated by **Deborah Melmon**

THE KANE PRESS / NEW YORK

For Vivien and Maeve, who have a lot of BIG ideas
—E.M.

Text copyright © 2013 by Eleanor May
Illustrations copyright © 2013 by Deborah Melmon

All rights reserved. No part of this book may be reproduced or transmitted in any
form or by any means, electronic or mechanical, including photocopying, recording,
or by any information storage and retrieval system, without permission in writing from
the publisher. For information regarding permission, contact the publisher through its
website: www.kanepress.com.

Library of Congress Cataloging-in-Publication Data

May, Eleanor.
Albert's bigger than big idea / by Eleanor May ; illustrated by Deborah Melmon.
p. cm. — (Mouse math)
"With fun activities!"
Summary: As the smallest mouse, Albert gets the smallest bag when he collects fruit in the People
Kitchen with his sister, Wanda, and Cousin Pete, but he wants to carry more than just a blueberry so
he makes a bigger bag. Introduces the concept of comparing sizes.
ISBN 978-1-57565-521-5 (library reinforced binding : alk. paper) — ISBN 978-1-57565-522-2 (pbk. :
alk. paper) — ISBN 978-1-57565-523-9 (e-book)
[1. Mice—Fiction. 2. Size—Fiction. 3. English language—Comparison—Fiction.] I. Melmon,
Deborah, ill. II. Title.
PZ7.M4513Alf 2013
[E]—dc23   2012025474

1 3 5 7 9 10 8 6 4 2

First published in the United States of America in 2013 by Kane Press, Inc.
Printed in the United States of America
WOZ0712

Book Design: Edward Miller

Mouse Math is a trademark of Kane Press, Inc.

Visit us online at **www.kanepress.com**

 Like us on Facebook
facebook.com/kanepress

Follow us on Twitter
@KanePress

Dear Parent/Educator,

"I can't do math." Every child (or grownup!) who says these words has at some point along the way felt intimidated by math. For young children who are just being introduced to the subject, we wanted to create a world in which math was not simply numbers on a page, but a part of life—an adventure!

Enter Albert and Wanda, two little mice who live in the walls of a People House. Children will be swept along with this irrepressible duo and their merry band of friends as they tackle mouse-sized problems and dilemmas. (And sometimes *cat-sized* problems and dilemmas!)

Each book in the **MOUSE MATH**™ series provides a fresh take on a basic math concept. The mice discover solutions as they, for instance, use position words while teaching a pet snail to do tricks or count the alarmingly large number of friends they've invited over on a rainy day—and, lo and behold, they are doing math!

Math educators who specialize in early childhood learning used their expertise to make sure each title would be as helpful as possible to young kids—and to their parents and teachers. Fun activities at the end of the books and on our website encourage children to think and talk about math in ways that will make each concept clear and memorable.

As with our award-winning Math Matters® series, our aim is to captivate children's imaginations by drawing them into the story, and so into the math at the heart of each adventure. It is our hope that kids will want to hear and read the **MOUSE MATH** stories again and again and that, as they grow up, they will approach math with enthusiasm and see it as an invaluable tool for navigating the world they live in.

Sincerely,

Joanne Kane

Joanne E. Kane
Publisher

Check out these titles in
MOUSE MATH:

Albert's Bigger Than Big Idea
Comparing Sizes: Big/Small

Count Off, Squeak Scouts!
Number Sequence

Mice on Ice
2D Shapes

The Right Place for Albert
One-to-One Correspondence

The Mousier the Merrier!
Counting

Albert's Amazing Snail
Position Words

Albert Keeps Score
Comparing Numbers

And visit
www.kanepress.com/
mousemath.html
for more!

Albert and his sister, Wanda, were going to the People Kitchen with their cousin Pete.

"Here's the plan," Cousin Pete said.
"Head straight for that big fruit bowl.
Snatch a piece of fruit.
And stuff it in your bag."

Cousin Pete handed out the bags.
His bag was **small**.
Wanda's was **smaller**.
Albert's was **smallest**.

small   **smaller**   smallest

"Why do I get the **smallest** bag?" Albert asked.

"You are the **smallest** mouse,"
his sister pointed out.

small   smaller   smallest

"Don't worry about the bags," Cousin Pete said.
"Worry about the cat."

Albert smiled.
"I may be the **smallest**, but I'm fast," he said.
"That cat will not catch me."

The three mice scrambled up onto the counter.
Cousin Pete popped a strawberry into
his **small** bag.
Wanda squeezed a grape into her **smaller** bag.

"Albert!" Wanda said.
"What in the world are you doing?"

Albert dropped a plum.

"I think that plum might be too **big** for you,"
Cousin Pete said.

"It's not too **big** for me," Albert gasped.
"But it is too **big** for my bag."

"I know which fruit will fit in your bag," Wanda said.
"The **smallest** fruit in the bowl—a blueberry!
It's just right for the **smallest** bag."

small   smaller   smallest

When they got home, Albert went into his room and shut the door.

Wanda knocked. "Want to play Cheesyland?"

"No, thank you," Albert said.

Their mother knocked.
"I made blueberry muffins with your blueberry."

"I'll eat one later, Mom," Albert said.

Finally Albert came out of his room.
"Look what I made!"

"That's a **big** bag," his mother said.

"*Very* big," Wanda said.

Albert said, "I hope it's big enough for a plum."

When they went back to the fruit bowl,
Albert took his **big** bag.

"Look, Albert," Wanda said.
"Your bag IS big enough for a plum!

"Albert?"

But Albert wasn't looking.

He was staring at a peach.
"Wow," he said. "It's even **bigger** than a plum."

Albert hardly spoke on the way home.

After dinner, he went back into his room
and shut the door.

"Look what I made now!" Albert said.

"That's even **bigger** than your other bag," his mother said.

Wanda said, "It's **bigger** than YOU."

The next day, they went back to the fruit bowl.
Wanda and Cousin Pete helped Albert
load the peach into his **bigger** bag.

"Okay, Albert, let's go," Cousin Pete said.
"Albert?"

Albert was staring at a watermelon.

"Wow," he said.
"That must be the **biggest** fruit in the whole world."

big   bigger   **biggest**

When they got home, Albert went
into his room and shut the door.

He stayed in there a long, long time.

"Ta-da!" Albert announced.

"My goodness," Albert's mother said. "That's the **biggest** bag yet."

"It's the **biggest** bag I've ever seen," Wanda said.

big   bigger   **biggest**

When Cousin Pete arrived, he stared at Albert's bag. "How are you going to get that bag all the way up to the counter?"

Albert hadn't thought about that.

"We can do it together!" Wanda said.

As Cousin Pete scampered ahead, Wanda and Albert dragged the bag across the kitchen floor.

A shadow fell across their path.
The cat!
It was very **big**.
As **big** as a watermelon, Albert thought.
But with a lot more teeth.

"Run, Albert!" Wanda said.

Albert stared at the cat.
He couldn't move.

The cat pounced.
Wanda yelled, "Albert!
Open the bag—and JUMP!"

Albert jumped one way.
Wanda jumped the other.

Then they scurried to safety.

"Cousin Pete was right," Albert said.
"That bag was too big."

"Too big for getting fruit," Wanda agreed.

"But just the right size to catch a cat!"

Albert's Bigger Than Big Idea supports children's understanding of **comparing sizes: big, bigger, biggest; small, smaller, smallest,** an important topic in early math learning. Use the activities below to extend the math topic and to reinforce children's early reading skills.

ENGAGE

Invite children to look at the cover illustration as you read the title aloud. Encourage them to tell what they think the story is about. Ask: *What do you think Albert wants? What might Albert's "bigger than big" idea be?* Record children's responses on a large sheet of paper and refer back to them after reading through the story for the first time.

LOOK BACK

After reading the story, ask questions such as the ones below to support children's comprehension of the plot and to reinforce the math concepts covered in the story.

▶ How many mice were in the story? Were they all the same size?
▶ Who was the smallest?
▶ Who carried the smallest bag? Why? Do you think that's fair? Why or why not?
▶ What three fruits did the mice bring back from their first trip? How big or small were the fruits?
▶ How did Albert feel about the fruit he brought home?
   Why do you think he felt that way?
▶ When Albert decided he wanted the plum, what did he do?
   Do you think this was a good plan? Why or why not?
▶ What other fruit did Albert manage to bring home?
▶ At the end of the story, who had the "biggest" bag?
▶ Why didn't Albert bring home the watermelon?
▶ How did Wanda help Albert at the end of the story?

🐭 TRY THIS!

Gather up different sized balls from around the home or school. Try to find, for example, a basketball, kickball, soccer ball, baseball, golf ball, and ping-pong ball (or other objects of comparable size). Have the children place them in size order from biggest to smallest.

Ask questions such as: *Which ball is the biggest? Smallest? How many are bigger than the soccer ball? How many are smaller than the baseball?*

Bonus! Gather up some bags such as grocery bags, plastic bags, lunch bags, and sandwich bags, and see which balls will fit into each of the bags. Have fun matching them up!

🐭 THINK!

Print out copies of the activity sheets at www.kanepress.com/mousemath-bigsmall.html. Have children look at the activity sheet with the different sizes of fruit on one side of the page and the containers on the other side of the page. Now have children draw lines to match up each piece of fruit with a container of corresponding size. Repeat the activity with the activity sheet that shows different sized mice and beds. Children may color in the pictures if they like!

Bonus! Give the children time to draw pictures of mice of different sizes. When the drawings are finished, have children cut out each mouse and line up the mice from smallest to biggest. Now have them line up the mice from biggest to smallest. Children may make up stories about their mice and share the stories if they wish.

Extra Challenge: Pair children up and have them mix all their pictures together and line them up by size order.

CONTRA COSTA COUNTY LIBRARY

◆ FOR MORE ACTIVITIES ◆

visit www.kanepress.com/mousemath-activities.html

31901055195509